For Vedant, who finds rainbows everywhere –
M.N

For Samuel, Noah, Poppy, Florence, George,
Hamilton, Dominic, Hudson, Eliza, Flynn & Caia, my great
nieces & nephews, with love –
J.L-F

First published in the United Kingdom in 2022 by Lantana Publishing Ltd.
www.lantanapublishing.com | info@lantanapublishing.com

American edition published in 2022 by Lantana Publishing Ltd., UK.

Text © Mamta Nainy, 2022
Illustration © Jo Loring-Fisher, 2022

The moral rights of the author and illustrator have been asserted.

Distributed in the United States and Canada by Lerner Publishing Group, Inc.
241 First Avenue North, Minneapolis, MN 55401 U.S.A.
For reading levels and more information, look for this title at
www.lernerbooks.com
Cataloging-in-Publication Data Available.

Hardback ISBN: 978-1-913747-74-9
eBook PDF: 978-1-913747-75-6
ePub3: 978-1-913747-76-3

Printed and bound in Europe
Original artwork created using mixed media, completed digitally

MAMTA NAINY

JO LORING-FISHER

RAINBOW HANDS

 Lantana

Playtime, studytime, naptime,
snacktime, storytime . . .

The days stretch on and on forever.

I like all the different times of the day.
But my favorite time is *painting-my-nails-time*.

I color my nails in the
many shades that Ma has
in those magical bottles.

She has one for every
mood and feeling.

When I wake from a lovely dream of magical fairies in faraway lands . . .

I paint my nails in the color of mystery.

A PERFECT PURPLE.

On the days I look at myself in the mirror and wonder, "What shall I be today?" . . .

I paint my nails in the color of possibilities.

AN INFINITE WHITE.

When I walk into the garden and spot velvety bees dancing from one smiling sunflower to the other . . .

I paint my nails in the blinding color of the sun.

A BRIGHTEST YELLOW.

There are days when the sky looks just like the sea.
The fluffy clouds come rolling, wave upon wave.

Then I paint my nails in the color of the sky-sea, sea-sky.

A SWIRLING BLUE.

In the afternoons when I play ball,
dig in the dirt or pick up worms . . .

I paint my nails to match
the mess and squelch.

A MOSSY GREEN.

On some nights, I gaze at the distant lights from the window of my room. They look like warm stardust sprinkled on the cool night sky.

Then I paint my nails in the color of their shimmer.

A GLOWING ORANGE.

At times, Papa frowns and says,
"What have you done to your nails?"

At other times, he says, "Why don't you
paint on paper instead?"

"It's fun painting my nails," I want to tell
him. "It makes my hands look beautiful!"

When I can't, I feel hot in my head.

I paint my nails the color of fire ants.

A FLAMING RED.

But when Dadaji, my grandpa, hugs me and says, "You're my colorful child, who I know will shine bright," . . .

I paint my nails in the color of the softest cotton candy.

A SWEETEST PINK.

And on those crazy days when I feel **SAD**, HAPPY,

ANGRY and **DREAMY** all at once, then . . .

I catch a **RAINBOW** in my hands!